DORRIE
and the Birthday Eggs
Patricia Coombs

Lothrop, Lee & Shepard Co. / New York

to Lena

This is Dorrie. She is a witch. A little witch. Her hat is always on crooked and her socks never match. She likes to be busy. She likes surprises.

It was the Big Witch's birthday. Dorrie and Gink, her black cat watched Cook making a cake. Cook mumbled and grumbled as she worked.

"I'll help," said Dorrie. "I'll stir."

"No!" said Cook. "Don't bother me. This cake has to be perfect to bring your mother good luck for a whole year."

Cook got out a bowl of eggs for the cake. She stepped on Gink's tail.

Gink jumped and yowled. So did Cook. The eggs
landed on the floor with a skrunch and a splish.

Cook was so mad she turned red and then purple.

"Don't worry," said Dorrie. "Gink and I will go to the Egg Witch and get some more."

Cook frowned. "Oh, all right. But hurry. And come right back. The cake must be baked before the Big Witch gets home."

Dorrie put on her cloak and her galoshes. She put the money for the eggs in her pocket.

Dorrie and Gink hurried out the back door and across the yard to the road. Up one hill they went and down another.

"Gink," said Dorrie, "I love to go on errands. I love birthdays and birthday cakes!"

Dorrie skipped. Then she hopped on one foot. She hopped and spun around in a circle.

She spun so fast she got dizzy and sat down with a thump in the road. One galosh flew off.

"Ow!" said Dorrie.

"Ow to you, too," said a high, thin voice. "I needed a new hat and this fits very well."

A skinny witch in a shawl all covered with patches was dancing around with Dorrie's galosh on her head.

As she danced she sang:
"Thinnever, Thinnever, Thinnever,
I gargle at midnight with vinegar;
My patches and plots catch every wretch
Who crosses the path of Thinnever Vetch."

"Stop!" yelled Dorrie. "Give that back." But the patchy witch had vanished.

"Oh, bother," said Dorrie. "Mother and Cook are going to be awfully mad at me for losing a galosh."

Gink sneezed. He was sniffing something in the road. It was the witch's patchy hat.

Dorrie stuffed the hat in her pocket. "Come on, Gink. That witch wasted a lot of our time."

They hurried down the road. At last they came to the sign that read:

EGGS FOR SALE. QUIET PLEASE
CHICKENS AT WORK.

Down the path and under the trees they ran. Dorrie's hat caught on a branch, and she tumbled backwards into the grass.

A big black chicken grabbed the hat and flew into the top branches.

"Oh, Gink," said Dorrie. "First my galosh, and now my best hat! Mother and Cook are going to be boiling mad!"

Dorrie brushed herself off. She put on the patchy witch's hat and knocked at the door.

She knocked and knocked. Big black chickens clucked and squawked all around.

"The Egg Witch isn't here, Gink. She must be out in the shed."

EGGS FOR
SALE
INQUIRE
WITHIN
The Egg Witch

They went to look. There were rows of nests with eggs. Some of them had black chickens sitting on them. The Egg Witch wasn't there.

"Oh dear," said Dorrie. "We'll just have to take the eggs and leave the money."

Dorrie took off her one galosh and filled it with eggs. She put the money in the nest.

"Come on, Gink, we've got to get home fast," said Dorrie.

It got darker and darker as they hurried along the road. A black shadow whooshed over their heads. They hurried even faster.

At last they saw the lights of their house. Into the yard they ran, and around to the kitchen.

Dorrie put down the eggs and opened the door.

"WHERE HAVE YOU BEEN ALL THIS TIME?" roared Cook.

"I went to the Egg Witch's, but—"

Cook frowned a very fierce frown. "The Egg Witch just flew here to see your mother. She said she didn't see you. Go to your room and get cleaned up, AT ONCE! The cake is ruined. I had to make it without eggs."

Dorrie stamped her foot. "A witch stole my galosh and a chicken took my. . . ."

"GO!" cried Cook.

Dorrie and Gink stamped upstairs. Dorrie put on her shoes and her second best hat. "Come on, Gink," sighed Dorrie. "Mother is going to be too mad to listen, just like Cook. But we'll try."

Down, down, down the stairs they went and into the parlor.

The Big Witch and the Egg Witch were having tea.

"Mother," said Dorrie, "It took me a long time because. . . ."

The Big Witch banged her teacup down. *"Not another word!* I have two headaches at once and I do *not* want to hear excuses. SIT DOWN!"

Dorrie and Gink sat down. Dorrie put her arms around Gink.

The Big Witch and the Egg Witch were hunched over the tea, talking.

"Well," the Egg Witch said, "I saw Thinnever Vetch's patchy old hat coming toward my door. I didn't answer her knock. I hid. Thinnever always means trouble."

The Big Witch nodded and stirred her tea.

"BUT," said the Egg Witch, "I didn't know *why* Thinnever was lurking around my place. The minute she left, I found out. I have an *enchanted* hen! One nest was full of silver coins instead of eggs! So I flew here as fast as I could. Of course, I locked up all my chickens first. Can you help me find out which one is enchanted?"

"Hmmm, I think so," the Big Witch said. "We must find out before Thinnever does."

"Yes!" cried the Egg Witch. "If Thinnever steals it, goodness knows what she will do. She is so mean to people, think how mean she'd be to a hen!"

The Big Witch rushed out of the parlor and came back with a pile of magic books.

"Mother," said Dorrie, "the Egg Witch got things mixed up . . ."

The Big Witch frowned and pointed her long pointy finger at Dorrie. "SILENCE!"

The Big Witch and the Egg Witch began looking at the books. "There must be a spell that will show us how to tell an enchanted hen from a plain one," muttered the Big Witch.

They frowned and scratched their heads and turned the pages faster and faster.

The Big Witch and the Egg Witch closed the books. The Egg Witch began to cry.

"Never mind," said the Big Witch. "Enchanted chickens must be rare. Come along, we will fly to the library. We will find the right spell there. You come too, Dorrie. I want to be sure you stay out of trouble. Hurry!"

Dorrie grabbed her cloak and followed the Big Witch and the Egg Witch out the door.

"WHERE ARE YOUR GALOSHES?" cried the Big Witch.

"A witch stole one and the other one is full of. . . ."

"Never mind!" said the Big Witch, "I don't want to hear excuses. Oh my head!"

Dorrie and Gink climbed on the broomstick behind the Big Witch. The Egg Witch got on her
broomstick and away they flew into the dark.

They swooped down in front of the library and rushed inside.

"We will each take a row of books," said the Big Witch. "And don't say a single word, Dorrie. We must not be disturbed."

Dorrie sighed. She sat down between the tall, gloomy shelves with a pile of books.

"This is silly, Gink," she whispered. "We could be home blowing up balloons if Mother would only listen to me." Dorrie went on turning pages.

Suddenly she stopped. There was a picture of Thinnever Vetch. Under the picture it said:

Troublemaker. Found on roads in late afternoon and at night. Expert in mischief and bad luck of all kinds. A patch torn from her shawl gives a person power over her. This is very hard to get. She turns herself into a clump of weeds when cornered.

"No wonder I had such bad luck on my errand, Gink," whispered Dorrie. "I'm not supposed to talk, but I can *write*. Come on, Gink."

Dorrie tiptoed over to the desk and got a piece of paper and a pencil. She was just about to go back when she saw something. Thinnever Vetch was watching the Big Witch and the Egg Witch through the library window! Dorrie heard a wicked chuckle. Then the face disappeared.

"That patchy old witch is up to no good," whispered Dorrie. "We've got to do something quick."

Dorrie wrote on the piece of paper:

> There isnent eny inchanted chiken.
> sombody tok the egs and left muny.
> sombody was waring this witchs
> pacthy hat becas a chiken tok hers.

Dorrie put the note in the book. She slid the book through the shelf toward the Big Witch.

The Big Witch picked it up. She opened to the page with the paper sticking out. She read the note. She scratched her head. She read it again. Then she spun around.

"I found the answer!" she cried.

"Oh, goody!" the Egg Witch yelled. "Which hen is enchanted? We are all going to be rich. Especially me. I'll build a gold hen house and. . . ."

The Big Witch stamped her foot. "Hush! A witch left the silver coins in that nest. A little witch." She pointed at Dorrie.

The Egg Witch looked at Dorrie. "She doesn't look much like a hen."

"Never mind that," said the Big Witch. "It's too hard to explain. We must find a spell that will stop Thinnever Vetch from playing tricks."

"Yes!" shouted the Egg Witch. "That would be more fun than being rich."

Dorrie tiptoed to the door and Gink went with her. The Big Witch and the Egg Witch were muttering as they read the spells.

"Come on, Gink," whispered Dorrie. "We are going to catch that bad-luck patchy witch ourselves. She ruined Mother's birthday cake, and stole my galosh. She's so busy spying on Mother and the Egg Witch we can take her by surprise."

They slipped outside. Dorrie peeked around a bush. Thinnever Vetch was hunched by the window, watching, and talking to herself.

"Ha, ha! By the time they find a spell and go flying off to mix it up, it will be too late! When they fly over Black Pond, the broomsticks will melt and down they'll drop like stones! And that dumpy little witch, wherever she is, she'll touch her galosh and WHOOF, KABOOM! She'll be in my cellar stirring up cauldrons of vinegar forever and ever. Oh, but I'm clever!"

As Thinnever cackled to herself, Dorrie went creeping up behind her. Gink slipped under the bush beside her. When Dorrie shouted, "NOW!" Gink leaped onto Thinnever's head.

"Eeeek!" Thinnever tumbled over backwards.

Dorrie grabbed her shawl and some patches just as Thinnever turned into a clump of weeds.

The Big Witch and the Egg Witch came running out of the library.

"Dorrie!" cried the Big Witch. "What is all this racket? What are you doing out here?"

Dorrie pointed to the clump of weeds.

"Thinnever Vetch turned herself and my galosh into a bunch of weeds."

The Big Witch shook her head, and sighed. "More of your stories! We all have a headache. We are going home and have tea again. We are going to forget about Thinnever Vetch. And hens. And galoshes."

The Big Witch and the Egg Witch started for their broomsticks.

"Stop!" yelled Dorrie. "There's a spell on them. They'll melt when we're over Black Pond! Take the spell off, Mother. Please!"

The Big Witch groaned. "Oh, all right. I'm too tired to argue!"

The Big Witch clapped her hands and spun around three times, saying:

> "If a spell on these is cast,
> Let it vanish, fast, fast, fast!
> Two times, two times, two times three,
> Let us homeward safely flee."

The Big Witch whirled to a stop. The folds of her cloak hung still. A cloud of red sparks hissed slowly from the tips of the broomsticks into the air.

"Oh, my," cried the Egg Witch. "Dorrie was right!"

The Big Witch stared at the sparks and turned pale.

"Oh, Dorrie," said the Big Witch. "I'm sorry I didn't listen to you. If you hadn't caught Thinnever we'd all be in the bottom of Black Pond right now."

Dorrie tugged at the Big Witch's sleeve.

"That's not all," she said. "Thinnever cast a spell on my other galosh. If Cook finds it before you fix it, she'll be in Thinnever's cellar forever."

They leaped on to the broomsticks and flew, fast as lightning, back to Dorrie's house.

Cook opened the kitchen door.
"Don't touch that galosh, Cook!" shouted Dorrie.

The Big Witch lifted her hands and closed her eyes. Around and around and around she spun, whispering a spell.

It was very quiet.

Suddenly a stream of sparks curled out of the galosh, sputtered and disappeared.

"That takes care of THAT," said the Big Witch.

Dorrie picked up the galosh and carried it inside. "Here are the eggs, Cook."

The Big Witch told Cook about the spell on the galosh.

"Oh dear," said Cook. "I'm sorry I yelled and didn't listen, Dorrie. I'd hate to be stirring cauldrons of vinegar forever and ever. I'll make a new cake. We'll call it Midnight Surprise Birthday Cake."

The Egg Witch snapped her fingers.

"Wait!" You won't need all the eggs for the cake." She took three of them and a handful of corn from her pocket. She tossed the eggs and corn into the air. She muttered and flapped her sleeves.

The eggs whirled around in a cloud over their heads, faster and faster. With a crack and a cluck, they landed on the floor.

The Big Witch laughed. "Hens! Three black birthday hens! Thank you, Egg Witch."

The black hens followed the Big Witch, Gink followed Dorrie, and they went into the parlor for tea.

Dorrie told them everything that had happened that afternoon when she went to get the eggs. This time they all listened.

Dorrie made the patches from Thinnever's shawl into a pincushion for the Big Witch. And the black hens laid lots of eggs forever after for Cook to make cakes with, and everybody was happy.